Th

a v a m p i r e t a l e

Monique Bowden Guice

Guice Publishing

Tallahassee, Fl

This book is a work of fiction. Names, characters, places, and incidents are either the product of the author's imagination or used fictitiously. Any resemblance to actual persons, living or dead, or to actual events or locales is entirely coincidental.

Copyright © 6 October 2015 by Monique Bowden Guice

The First (a vampire tale)

All rights reserved. No part of this book may be reproduced in any form without the expressed written permission of the publisher except by a reviewer.

The book is published by Monique Bowden Guice

Guice Publishing
3502 Chatelaine Ct
Tallahassee, Fl 32308
850-445-0409

A company based on faith, hope and love

Email us at: guicepublishing@gmail.com
Visit our website at: http://mbguice.webs.com/
Cover designed by: Gwendolyn M. Michelle Evans

This book is dedicated to all those that helped and encouraged me along the way.

You paid it forward.

The Beginning

Aubrey saw them as soon as the door of the diner opened. The female with thick black tresses cascading over her shoulders was dressed in a modest denim skirt with ruffles and a matching jacket with a scarf wrapped around her neck. The male with the same black hair was dressed in navy baller shorts, a white wife beater, and flip flops. There was no mistaking. Vampires.

A warning growl gathered at the base of Aubrey's throat, low but loud enough for every wolf, if they were paying attention, to pick up. He checked the clock. It was barely seven, but the sun had already gone down. It would be at least another hour before the pack enforcers showed up.

What the hell did vampires want here? Werewolves and Vampires had nothing in common. Aubrey couldn't think of one reason for them to step across his threshold.

Surely they smelled the scent of wolf throughout the diner. Even human customers noticed a "wild smell" in the diner. He covered with the humans by saying it was the wild boar he served on the menu. Boar that Aubrey and his pack hunted and brought down when they were in their wolf form – that part they kept to themselves.

But then again, he didn't really know how well vamps could smell. He didn't know anything about vampires at all. All he was sure of was their coming to his place of business made him uncomfortable.

He heard Carla greet them with a curt, "Can I help you?"

"I would like to see the pack master," the female said.

"Excuse me?" Carla flipped her bleached blonde hair out of her eyes. The young female wolf didn't mind letting the vamps know how much she disliked having them enter their establishment.

"The pack master, please," the male said impatiently.

Carla yelled over her shoulder, "Yo, Aubrey, someone here to see ya." She walked over to the counter where another young woman stood wearing the same Timberwolves uniform of black shorts and a red T-shirt.

The din in the room softened as several of the patrons and workers turned to see who the young woman was yelling to.

Aubrey's long legs covered the distance to the front faster than usual. He didn't want vampires in his establishment and was determined to get them off the property as soon as possible. As he neared the two, he couldn't help but notice the shapely, dark-haired woman. She had large black eyes fringed by long, black lashes. Her lips were full and kissable. His eyes immediately landed on her breasts, which were hidden under a scarf. He could see the way her waist tucked in to round out into curvy hips and thighs. As a man, he liked that. Oddly enough, the werewolf in him liked what he saw as well. She could really be attractive if the woman was not already dead.

"We don't have donors here." Aubrey made his voice strong with the authority of being the pack master of the Timberwolves. He had to push his thick and unruly coffee-colored hair out of his eyes. His brown eyebrows knitted together as he reminded himself for the hundredth time today he needed a haircut. His nose flared as the werewolf in him tried to pick up the scent of the vampires. Nothing. Rubbing the stubble that covered his square jaw line, he remembered what that meant.

Old. They were old.

From experience, he knew the newer the vamp, the easier it was to pick up the death scent. It was too faint for most humans to notice. Werewolves, on the other hand, had a hundred thousand times the ability to scent than humans did. Now that he was closer, he tried again to smell them. He got nothing but the smell of aftershave and perfume.

His other half, the wolf, was confused. His suspicion aroused, the wolf in him crouched under his skin.

"Pack master?" the female asked in a polite voice. Her voice had a musical lilt to it.

Annoyed that he couldn't scent them, Aubrey said, "Yeah. What can I do for you folks? Like I said, we don't have donors here. We don't normally get your kind. I guess you can figure out the reason."

Both vamps gave a modest nod.

"We come in peace. May we sit? We have an urgent matter to discuss." The female looked him in the eye. Her eyes, black like coal, sparkled like diamonds.

Every muscle in his body went on high alert. What urgent matter? They didn't know him. He was sure he didn't know them. What could be so important? One thing he was certain, he could not show any fear or weakness. He was pack master, leader of the Timberwolves; they feared no man or beast. He shrugged. "Yeah, we can sit, but don't try any of that Vampire bullshit. I can't be hypnotized."

He pointed to the smaller section of the restaurant at a round table in the corner. It was his usual place for meetings in the diner.

Aubrey stood in front of a round table and extended his arm for the vampires to go to the back of the table. That put them close to the glass wall that faced the parking lot. Aubrey liked this corner. Two walls were glass. In the evening, the glass acted as a mirror that helped him see what was going on behind him while he was still able to see cars moving in the parking lot. Besides, in the event this thing turned ugly, it would be better to have them boxed against the wall.

"You are not the shaman or a warlock? Perhaps a witchdoctor," the male said, rooted in place.

Aubrey straightened. "We don't have any of those."

"You have a witch then?" The female took the chair next to the one where he stood.

"We don't have one of those either."

The vampires stared.

"Is that it? That's what you wanted to know from me?" Aubrey looked at them for a few seconds. When they didn't respond, he raised his palms to them. "I'm busy. If that's it, I'll get back to what I was doing." The faster he got them out of his diner, the better.

"I know our kind and yours don't often get along, but there is a threat to you and yours. Perhaps you can spend another minute," the female said. She turned sideways in her chair and crossed her legs, displaying a pair of strappy black sandals with a wedge heel. Her legs were smooth and short with a gold chain around her right ankle. She made her intentions very clear that she was in no hurry to leave.

The male vamp took a seat next to the female.

Freakin' vamps think they run everything. Aubrey knew they had the rest of the world fooled into thinking they were just misunderstood. He knew they were a bunch of sneaks that used trickery to get what they wanted. Now, he had a choice to make. Call the pack together and throw them out, or listen to what they had to say. He looked around and counted the humans in the diner, more than half of the patrons. That made the decision for him. Aubrey turned a chair around and straddled the seat. "What's this threat?"

"The woman called you Aubrey," the female vamp stated.

Aubrey shrugged. There was something in her speech pattern, the inflections in her words. Not really an accent but he needed to pay close attention.

"I am Night and this is my brother, Day. We have followed magic here to this place. We need to find the witch or shaman that cast the spell."

"Like I said, we don't have a witch or shaman. The last one we had died about a year, year and a half ago."

Aubrey noticed Night and Day glance at the door. In the reflective glass, he watched as two more vampires came inside. The two new vamps didn't wait for the hostess. Instead, they went to the opposite side of the restaurant. Two more vamps followed the first two and came toward Aubrey. They walked to the corner behind Day, then took a seat at the table across from them.

These two were the same—tall, dark-skinned, with black hair flowing freely around their faces. Their black eyes were flat, eyelashes thick, and they carried themselves like they owned the place.

Aubrey eyed them all suspiciously and gave a low growl of warning.

"These are my brothers, Dark and Morning."

"I can see that. You all look just alike." It was clear to Aubrey that these vamps had the same human blood line.

They were as tall as Aubrey, who knew his own height was six-foot-four, and they were just as lean. They had inky black hair with copper-colored skin, black eyes, and hard angled faces. The female was shorter but her coloring was the same.

Aubrey's thirteen-year-old sister, Emma, came behind him carrying a tray laden with glasses of ice water. "Would y'all like a glass of ice water?" she cheerily sang.

"Witch!" Morning hissed followed by Day. "Witch!" Their dark eyes squinted as they leaned closer to the child.

Aubrey stood up, making his chair topple, his first instinct to protect Emma, his youngest sister. He could not allow these undead freaks to put their hands on her.

He took a protective stance between Emma and the vampires. His muscles tightened and his body bent in anticipation of the change. Suddenly, he felt a wind at his back. He allowed his peripheral vision to check the glass and realized that the two vampires from the other end of the diner had flanked him at the rear.

The wolf inside him begged, demanded him to change into his stronger, more dangerous half. His hands yanked the apron from around his neck and pulled at the buttons on his shirt. He felt the muscles in his face start to elongate and his teeth sharpen.

He had to contain himself. There were humans inside the diner, families with children that could be hurt. If he changed in front of them, there would be hell to pay—not only for him, but for all his kind.

Werewolves were not like the vampires. Werewolves wanted to be hidden in the shadows and public displays were forbidden. To be pack master, he needed to remain in control, regardless of the situation. He knew his wolves loved to fight as much as he did and the smell of fresh blood would only feed their fury. He expected no less from the vampires.

Aubrey fought his beast to bring it back under control.

Emma tried to get out of the way of Aubrey's long legs but got caught in the tangle. In an attempt to keep her balance, she lost her footing and tripped. Glasses, water, and chunks of ice flew into the air and crashed to the floor. The sound of glass breaking sliced above the din of the diner, creating a hush over the place as everyone turned to stare.

"I'm sorry," Emma said, and scurried around Aubrey with a towel she produced from her back pocket.

"Emma, get over here." Aubrey grabbed his sister and brought her close to him. He had to protect her. He let a loud growl escape; alerting the other wolves in the bar their help was needed.

Every head, human and other, craned at the sound: a wild animal, an angry wolf close by, indoors, warning, and ready for attack. Human mothers gathered their children close while the fathers placed themselves in front of their families.

The werewolves readied themselves for a fight.

"Let me go!" Emma squirmed to get away. "I'm a wolf, too. I can protect myself."

Sure she was a wolf ... a wolf that had not had her first transformation. Even though she was stronger than most human children her age, she was still weak for a werewolf. She'd only just turned thirteen the week before and her body hadn't caught up with her attitude.

Todd, Nick, and Darla crowded the smaller section of the diner. Darla stripped off her jacket in preparation for a fight.

Unconcerned, Night remained seated, making a show out of admiring her sandals as she adjusted one strap and then another. "Please," she said, sounding bored. "We only want to talk to the child. I promise no harm will come to either of you."

"Why should I trust a vampire?" Aubrey asked between clenched teeth.

Night gave a mischievous smile. "We are six vampires and there are only, what, thirty of you wolves here. If we wanted to hurt you, you all would be dead by now. We just want to talk." Absentmindedly, she brushed a chunk of ice from her lap. "Please sit. I insist."

"How are you gonna insist on anything in my place?" Aubrey made it a statement. He wanted them to know that he was still in charge in his own establishment.

Night chose to ignore him. Instead, she turned her attention to the little girl. "Hello, little witch," she said in a soft tease while the index finger on her right hand lightly tapped the tip of Emma's nose.

"You're Vampires," Emma said with excitement. "And you came because of me?"

Aubrey grabbed for Emma in order to get her closer to him.

Emma backed away from her brother into one of the vampires. She looked up into the vampire's dark, handsome face and smiled. "Excuse me."

The vampire nodded to her and helped her keep her balance. Grateful, Emma gave him her best smile.

"Emma, get back in the kitchen," Aubrey ordered, his voice rising through his clenched teeth. "You don't have any business out here."

Emma bucked. Aubrey wasn't surprised. She was like her mother—a stubborn, defiant, Puerto Rican werewolf that refused to be tamed. Since last week, when she turned thirteen, Emma had changed. It was like becoming a teenager came with a personality transplant. Bouncing her bushy pony tail, Emma said, "You told me to bring water to every customer. And you weren't going to pay me for the people I missed. I ain't gonna mess up the money I'm supposed to get 'cause I didn't do it." She looked at the female vampire, who was still seated, and said in a syrupy voice, "Would you like some water, Miss?"

"Emma!" Aubrey roared loud enough for the entire restaurant to hear him. He didn't care how foolish he sounded—he had to protect her. In the dark of the window, he could see customers lining up to pay and make the exodus to the parking lot. More pack mates—Chester, John and Shannon—gathered behind the vampires at his back.

"Enough," Night said. "Sit." She eyed each of her brothers, who took their time sitting. "We come in peace. There will be no fighting."

Night smiled at Emma. "Please, may I have the water now?"

"Yes, ma'am. I'll be right back." Emma hurried off. She took the long way around to avoid contact with Aubrey.

Aubrey glared at each vampire in turn. His restaurant was a public place; there was no way to rescind their invitation and make them leave. Besides, they could come back at any time and bring more vamps with them.

This thing could turn into an all-out war. He didn't want to fight, but if he had to, that was okay by him.

"What do you want?" he snapped. He didn't care he was being rude. He wanted them gone. Motioning for Carla and Tina to come clean the water and broken glass from the floor, Aubrey glared at the vampires, which allowed his wolf to rise just a bit more.

The corners of Night's mouth curved slightly. "These are my brothers Day, Earth, Sky, Morning, and Dark. We have come seeking your witch to remove the spell she has cast. I have tried several times to counter the spell, but it keeps coming back. I fear for her if she does not stop casting her spell."

"You lay a finger on my sister and I will kill you," Aubrey warned, his tone matter of fact.

"We do not take kindly to threats." Morning leaned forward with his fangs partially extended.

"No more," Night said sharply to her brother. Her attention was on a female werewolf at Aubrey's back. Darla. She would be harder to control, more than the men that stood behind Aubrey.

"Pack Master, we would not have broached ..."

"How do you even know Emma?" Darla demanded with clenched fists, her body slightly bent. The growl in her voice was barely contained. "What makes you think she cast this spell?"

"We do not know Emma." Night draped her elbows over the back of the chair. "We followed the magic to this place. When she speaks, the magic is on her lips. It fills the air. I can see it. Do you see it, Brother?"

Morning nodded, his focus never leaving the wolves.

"That's ridiculous. She's just a kid. She don't know nothin' 'bout magic," one of the werewolves said, pulling up a chair to take a seat.

"That is one of the things we would like to make sure of. Is she child?" Night asked her brother. "Or is she crone?"

"She is child," Earth said. "I smell no crone in her. Not even one reincarnated." Earth leaned back in his chair. His long legs extended from the table and he folded his hands over his stomach.

Aubrey recognized the vamp's body language as a taunt. He knew the rest of the pack did too. He sent a low warning for them not to take the bait.

"Nor did I sense any crone in her." Night extended her hand to Aubrey. "Pack Master, we must speak. Your little witch is attempting to wake a very old vampire. For now, I have a spell in place to block her spell, but her magic is pure with daggers and chips away at my counter spell. If she should succeed in waking this vampire, he will come to her.

It is dangerous to wake a vampire; even more dangerous to wake him by magic."

"No dead fanger is gonna take one of our pups. You just let him try," Darla growled.

Aubrey silenced Darla with a glance. He needed to listen carefully to what the female vamp was saying. He was at a loss. His wolf was trapped because it couldn't scent the vampires and know what they were truly up to. Everything had a scent. Everything. Not having a scent mocked the wolf. The wolf caught what he could from these creatures. Emotion. From the woman, he was able to pick up an air of sincerity, possibly concern?

He would not allow his prejudice to cloud his judgment, especially not when it concerned Emma. For that reason alone, he would find the strength to maintain his head.

"Darla, I got this," Aubrey said to the female wolf. He could scent her. R*age, mistrust, hatred* – ricocheted throughout the room.

Aubrey and Darla bore holes into each other before she lowered her eyes and relaxed a micro fraction. He'd have to keep an eye on her.

Aubrey was pissed. He couldn't afford to be distracted by trying to control the tempers of his pack. He needed to focus on these vamps, all six of them. That is where his attention needed to be. He needed to find a way to get them out of there without incident, without them harming or taking Emma. Aubrey righted the toppled chair, spread his legs and straddled the chair again. He placed his hands on the back of the chair and stared. He decided on something he had little or no experience with—diplomacy. He gentled his voice and tried to make his face expressionless. "That's my little sister and we don't practice magic in our family, none of us. I'm sure you've made a mistake."

"No one wakes a vampire unless they wish for death, and a vampire of this magnitude cannot be controlled unless the person summoning him possesses even more powerful magic. Even then, he will fight the magic. He has the knowledge and the power. This is why we have come. If she were a crone, we would have killed her already. But an innocent? With magic strong and pure. I am … confused."

* * * *

Emma returned with another tray of water. Night took the tray from her and handed it to Aubrey. She sat Emma on the table. "Emma, my little witch, you are trying to wake a vampire. Why?" Night asked in a casual voice.

Though Emma made no protest at the vampire's touch, Aubrey felt the hairs on his arms bristle.

"I'm not trying to wake anyone." Emma's answer was shy, nervous.

Aubrey could smell the lie.

"There is no need to be afraid. We are not angry. But we must know what your intentions are." Night gave her a reassuring smile.

Emma lowered her head. She chewed her bottom lip, then the top. Keeping her head down, she looked from Night to Aubrey.

Night watched her without expression or movement of any kind.

Aubrey glared at Emma, his nose and mouth twitching with impatience as he sought out her scent. He didn't like what he found. *Excitement, nervousness, fear, agitation, pride.* "Emma," he bellowed.

Emma blurted, "I just wanted to win."

"Of course, you did, darling. We all want to win. But what is it you wanted to win?" Night asked gently.

"The prize money for writing the best essay. I figured if I could get the real vampire here, I could ask him questions and that would make my report the best because it wouldn't just be what *would* I ask him, but what *did* I ask him. And then, he could come to the presentation with me and show everyone and I'd win. See?"

Night didn't see. With raised eyebrows, she turned to Aubrey for clarification. "Pack Master?"

"It's a school thing," he said.

All the vampires said, "Oh."

"You wanted to ask a vampire questions?" Night coaxed the girl to continue.

"Not just any vampire. There are so many now there is nothing special about them. I want the very first vampire but I didn't know who he was or where to find him. So, I found this spell online that said it was to get someone to come to you and do your bidding's. "

Aubrey yowled; his fist hit the table in frustration. "My God, Emma, do you have any idea how dangerous that is? You could freaking get yourself killed. You just wait 'til dad and your mom find out about this." He shook his head, mortified that she had even made an attempt at such a thing.

"He's gonna do my bidding." Emma wagged her neck. "I was gonna be all right. Except, he didn't come."

Disgust dripped from Aubrey's tongue. "And you'd better be glad he didn't. A vampire! What were you thinking?" He could feel his blood pressure rise. Being responsible for this girl was going to be the death of him. No way in hell did he ever want a daughter of his own.

"Well, he didn't come 'til now. Which one of you is him? Who was first?" Emma looked around.

Night gathered the girl's hands. "We are all the first, but there is one even more so. We have come on his behalf. Emma, my little witch, it took very specific magic to do what you have done. Where did you get this vampire's name?"

"See, that's just it. I didn't know his real name. I knew it couldn't be Dracula, but I looked him up just to make sure. My research said Dracula's family was cursed and the

28

Devil took a scholar from the family every 10th generation and the Dracula we know was the one the devil took in that generation? I mean, what's that? If he'd been born a generation later, there would not have been any Dracula?"

"Then I read another account on how the first vampire was made that said after Dracula found his wife dead, he drank blood, cursed God, and died. After that, they started to refer to him as vampire. There are no details on how the curse affected him. Just that they started to call him vampire. That still didn't make sense to me. It was like something was being left out. I wanted more details 'cause I knew Ms. Reese was gonna question my fact checking skills."

Emma looked around and took notice that everyone was listening to her. She liked being the main attraction of the evening.

"I read the Vampire Bible and it said some guy named Ambrogio was the first, but his story had a lot to do with the Greek gods and mythology stuff. I knew that was not true even if they did put it in the Vampire Bible. Then, I read a story about the vampire Lilith, which made even less sense. It said she got kicked out the Garden of Eden 'cause she didn't want to sleep under Adam. And she traded going back to heaven to become the mother of all demons. WTF?"

"Watch your language, little girl," Aubrey grumbled.

Emma paid Aubrey no attention and kept talking. "Who'd make the choice to be mother to all demons over going to heaven? And who would want to sleep under some guy? I guess if they were gonna do it or something." She lowered her voice and whispered, as if she was embarrassed to say the words.

Night's laugh filled the little room. "Yes, if they were going to do it or something," she repeated.

Clearly, this was amusing to her. Frustrated, Aubrey snapped. The wolf inside him needed to chastise the girl. The male in him needed to feel he could command something.

"Hey, you watch your mouth, young lady. You know you are too young for that kind of talk."

Entertained, Night said, "No, Pack Master. She is right. WTF! You are a wise young lady. Tell me more."

All the vampires leaned in, giving Emma their undivided attention. Even Aubrey's pack mates were interested. Aubrey couldn't help but notice these vamps were ignoring everyone except Emma. He tried to relax a bit, but he couldn't. His wolf was edgy. Discreetly, he loosened another button on his shirt and eased his feet from his shoes. He should be ready in case he needed to change to his stronger wolf form.

"Well, my assignment was to be the paparazzi," Emma said, beaming. Clearly she liked the assignment as much as the attention she was getting. "To interview the most interesting person I could think of, living or dead. I had to tell how I got the story: what tactics I would use, who I would interview, and the questions I would ask. Sooo, I figured I

31

would interview the first ever vampire and find out how he or she was made and how they got that way."

"All the news and talk shows say that a vampire can't have a baby, so they are not born, that a person is made into a vampire. I didn't really know who it was or where to find them.

"Pam said—that's my friend, Pam. Well, she said her cousin, Mandy, had a friend named Candy who said maybe we could send a call out to the universe and see what we get. So, we were looking online on how to call to the universe and I found the spell to get someone to come to you and do your bidding chant. I followed the instructions, and now, here you are."

The vamps looked at each other. Aubrey could tell they were having trouble following the logic of a thirteen-year-old girl.

It was the female vampire, Night, who took the lead. "Very interesting, little witch. What name for the vampire did you use in the spell?"

"I didn't know what name to use. I just said the first ... the first one ever."

"Clever little witch," Morning said.

"Clever, indeed," Night said. "Emma, darling, where is this spell? I'd like to see it, if you don't mind."

"Oh, I know it by heart. Eno salma hue tri ..."

Without warning, Night slapped her hands together in a loud clap a bare centimeter from Emma's mouth. "No, you must not say those words. The magic still clings to them. Do you understand? Those are words of strong magic, and every time you say them, you are recasting the spell."

Emma fell backward out of the way of Night's hand clap with the speed of a true supernatural being. Just as fast, Aubrey was on his feet grabbing his sister to pull her to safety. Instead of accepting her brother's assistance, Emma slapped at his hands and scrambled out of his grasp.

Aubrey's temper flared. The little minx thought this was some sort of game, but it didn't surprise him. Emma never did what was expected of her. He wanted to shake some sense in her. She was playing with vampires.

Before Aubrey could complete his thought, two vampires, Morning and Day, took to the air with blurring speed and became streaks of black and blue. Their movement was so fast, it was impossible for Aubrey to track them, and he was the best tracker in the pack.

Aubrey's eyes blazed rich amber, the wolf in him barely contained under his skin. He had no idea what the vamps were doing. The display was startling, unnerving. It made him realize that his own superior speed could be easily matched by these vamps if things should go wrong. He was never one to run from a fight. He had every confidence his wolf would find an effective means of attacking when the need arose.

A blink of an eye later, the vamps were seated in their original spots. They watched the air with the other vampires with expectant eyes, except the one called Morning. He leaned against the wall, his arms casually folded against his chest, the slightest hint of fang showing ... his gaze unblinking on Aubrey.

"The words had to be recaptured. If they were allowed to continue, they would have headed for their target, like heat-seeking missiles," Night cooed.

Aubrey checked the wolves behind him. Their eyes were ablaze with their other nature rising, ready to defend.

The air hung heavy with uneasiness, mistrust, envy, hatred, and fear.

Again, Aubrey encouraged his pack to maintain control. He was sure no one in his pack expected the vampires to move with such blinding speed, and his pack had to be struggling to control their wolves the same as he was. If one of them changed to their other form, they all would change, including him. That would be a clear, undeniable challenge to the vamps that he was sure they would answer. Blood would be shed. Emma would be hurt and so would his human employees. There was no way to tell if the fight could be contained inside the building. If the fight happened to spill outside, there was no telling the damage that could be done.

  Aubrey followed the scent of fear to Tina. She was a young, small wolf with a weak blood line who didn't have her full wolf strength yet; but she would stand with her pack. In the reflective glass, they locked eyes and he silently sent her his courage. He'd protect her, just as he would Emma. Tina was pack. He wanted her to know he'd let nothing happen to her. More importantly, she had to remember that as a pack, they didn't show fear to anyone.

Tina drew her mouth tight, forcing a mask on her young face. She pulled her posture straight and tore her eyes from Aubrey's reflection.

"What was all of that?" Aubrey demanded of the vampires.

"How many times have you said the words?" Dark asked from the shadow of the corner.

Emma resettled herself on the table. "I don't know, lots of times. I had to practice reading them and pronouncing the words correct, or at least, what I think is correct."

"Did you say them more than five times?" Dark asked.

"Way more."

"More than twenty-five?"

"Easy."

"Does not matter at this point. We need the words and find the incantation to counter the original spell," Dark said. "Emma, can you write the words for us?"

"I don't have to. I can get my computer and show you the report." Without hesitation, she hopped from the table and hurried off. "Don't go anywhere. I'll be right back," she called over her shoulder.

"She is adorable. I would love to keep her," Night said wistfully.

"That's not gonna happen." Aubrey growled.

"Pack Master." Night lifted her eyebrow. "You take me seriously? Surely, the tales of baby thieves holds more truth for your kind than ours."

Aubrey shrugged. "I'm gonna be honest with you. I don't know our history like I should." He pointed to the last spot where Emma sat. "All I do know is that's my baby sister and I'll die before any harm comes to her. I hope I make myself clear."

Night gave an ever-so-slight nod. "I know we have no real reason to trust each other, but is it possible that you could consider for one moment that we are as I say? That we have no interest or desire to hurt the girl? A shaman or witch would not have fared as well. We would have demanded the removal of the spell at once and killed them afterward for casting the spell in the first place."

They would have killed them afterward. Aubrey rolled the words over in his mind. Yeah, sure they came in peace all right. He considered the statement for a second and knew she was telling him the truth. "And you are not going to do that ... kill Emma?" He held his breath. If she answered wrong, this little gathering was about to be over.

* * * *

"She is a child, Pack Master," Night said in a soothing tone that sounded human. "Throughout the years my brother, Sky, has been attracted to human women with young children. He has married the women and raised the children as his own. He is a great, grandfather many times over. We have often found his children to be a great source of joy and entertainment. We would never hurt one of them. We have never hurt any child."

Aubrey grunted. That was neither a yes or no. "Now, you're gonna tell me all vampires like kids."

"Honestly, Pack Master." Night gave a slight shake of the head. "Do all humans like children? Do all werewolves? Can you swear to me that no werewolf has ever harmed a child? I know from personal experience that is not true. We are just as individual as you are. There are those of our kind that believe the blood of the innocent is sweeter. Then, there are those who love the blood of the evildoers, saying it is tastier. Because one is a vampire does not mean that it is evil, no more than being a werewolf makes one evil."

"What exactly makes a vampire evil?" Todd asked from behind Aubrey.

"If a person is evil in life, they will be evil in death. You cannot change what you are at the core of your being. I'm sure it will be the same for your kind."

Shannon snapped. "We are born this way and we don't have to kill to live."

"No, your kind has never had to kill to live. And yet, your kind does kill. Isn't that why your kind has *chosen* to stay a secret? To stay in the shadows?" Night finally answered Aubrey's question with infinite patience. "No. We will not hurt Emma. Not this night or any other."

Aubrey found her words relaxing, her velvet smooth tone wrapping around him. He still needed to be sure nothing was going to happen to Emma. "And what if this spell can't be lifted or changed. What harm is going to come to Emma, then?"

Everything was quiet for a moment. Night looked thoughtfully from one of her brothers to the next before she answered. "If we cannot reverse the spell, we will protect her. We will stay close to her. My father will recognize us and will not hurt one of us. Emma will need another spell to give him direction. Until that spell is cast, he will be under the compulsion of the spell that calls to him now."

Aubrey considered his predicament. This vampire sat with him talking. Talking. She made no demands. Made no threats. Though he couldn't scent her, Aubrey could feel himself relaxing. There was something in her words. No, in her voice, that was soothing. Satin and silk rolled into cooling jell that relaxed him, and wrapped him in warmth. He wanted to believe her. He did believe her.

Aubrey bellowed over his shoulder, "Tina, bring my food." To the vampires he said, "We got bottled blood. The beverage company and the laws require we carry it. You guys want any?"

"I'd like some," Night said. "Would you heat it in a bowl and bring a spoon?"

"Coors," was echoed by the remaining vamps.

Tina raised her eyebrows and headed back to the kitchen to place the order.

Less tense now, Aubrey looked past the mirror images in the window. Outside, a fog swirled around the parking lot. It was thick, slightly green, and menacing. It pushed against the window like it had a life, trying to get in.

A moment later, the waitress was back with a tray laden with dishes. Tina placed Coors in front of the vamps. In front of Aubrey, she announced the food items on the dishes. "I got ya rare T-bone steak with a loaded baked potato, half rotisserie chicken, yellow rice, and a mug of beer. It's all hot. Cook kept it warm for ya, and I didn't top off your beer. I got you a new one. Anything else I can get you? "

"Fork."

Tina reached into her pocket and pulled out a packet of flatware wrapped in a napkin. She placed a bowl of the red liquid in front of Night, and then pulled out another napkin of rolled flatware. "Enjoy," she said and walked to the edge of the room.

Aubrey scented Tina again. Less fear, a little suspicion.

Aubrey wasted no time digging into his steak. He sawed off a large hunk, rolled it around in the bloody juices on the plate, and shoved it in his mouth. As he chewed, he watched Night unroll the flatware with delicate fingers and place the napkin in her lap. Carefully, she scooped up a spoonful of the vile red fluid, placed it in her mouth, and then dabbed at the corners of her mouth with the napkin.

He grunted in amusement. He was eating dinner with a vampire. How the hell did that happen?

The female vamp reached for the salt and pepper. "O negative," Night said. "It's the most common blood in humans, but when they bottle it, it's a bit bland. Manufactured blood does not have the actual flavor of fresh blood. I find that spices help."

Aubrey nodded. Something about her was – cute. "What other spices do you use?"

"If I want Italian, I add oregano. If I want Chinese, I add soy."

Looking deeper, Aubrey saw that her inky black hair had pools of blue, red, and purple in it. He liked her skin, smooth, flawless. She had eyes that were happy and bright. And her lips were so full and sensuous. He could imagine all sort of interesting things he could do with that mouth. He smiled.

"You are amused, Pack Master?"

"That isn't the word that's in my mind."

"What is the word in your mind, Pack Master?"

Aubrey liked how she said Pack Master. It was kind of musical and sexy. "So, you're saying that the blood from ethnic people has the flavor of that nationality?"

Night placed her spoon in her bowl and folded her hands in her lap, back perfectly straight. "Yes, that is what I'm saying."

That simple action had his wolf crouching, waiting in anticipation. He studied her. Her large black eyes held a trace of deviousness. He hadn't had much experience with vampires, but he had plenty of experience with women. She was playing. He decided he'd play. "Mexicans taste like?"

"Tacos." She had a real smile, one that showed gleaming white teeth and reached from the corners of her mouth to her eyes.

"And black people taste like?"

She giggled. "Chicken."

He laughed hard and deep. A full, belly laugh. His laughter increased when he realized that she was laughing with him. He caught their reflection in the mirrored glass for an instant before he saw the reflection of his pack mates behind him. The wolf scented his pack mates: *surprise, disgust, hostility, frustration, bitterness.* Aubrey regained his pack master's persona.

Night also stopped laughing and looked at her brothers, who were staring at her. "What?" she demanded.

"You dog-gone right, what!" Shannon snapped from behind Aubrey. "Are we supposed to be watching your freakin' date?"

"You can leave at any time, Shannon," Aubrey bellowed.

The female wolf shrank back in her seat. Anger and disgust permeated the air around her.

A breathless Emma returned with her arms full. She shoved dishes out of her way. On the table, she laid a laptop, folder, three books, and her cell phone. "My teacher likes us to show our work, so I have to keep everything. She says that's the way it is when you brainstorm. You take all the ideas and then you sort through them to see which ones will work for you. Then, you develop them into points to be expanded and expounded on."

Aubrey, Night, and Day gathered to look at the papers Emma was pulling from the folder.

"Very interesting," Night said to Emma. To Day, she asked, "Do you see anything?"

"No," Day responded.

"I have no idea what I'm looking at," Aubrey said.

"See, here are the stories I downloaded about who is supposed to be the first. Like I said, they didn't make sense. So, I thought, 'How you can get someone that might be dead to come back and talk.' Then, me and Pam had a séance. Nothing happened. Then, we thought a voodoo woman could do it. So, we called the one that advertises on the radio, but the prices started from five hundred dollars to over a thousand dollars. Since I don't have that much money, I decided to try it myself. So, I looked up spells on the Internet and decided on this one." She handed Night a piece of paper.

"We are required to have at least three examples or attempts. Here are the ones I made."

Morning took the paper and examined it. "This is too simple. Not much power in it at all."

"That's what I thought. Then, I tried this one next." She handed them another piece of paper.

"This is stronger," Morning said. "But I don't see how it's working either. Did you combine them?"

"Yes. And then I found this one." She handed him another piece of paper.

Morning's hands instantly recoiled. The paper floated to the floor.

Emma picked it up. "What?"

"That's the spell with power. What website did you get it from?"

"That one didn't come off the web. I got it from this book." She moved her English and Grammar books to reveal an old, worn, leather book.

Morning said, "Turn to the page."

Without hesitation, Emma flipped the pages and handed the book to Morning.

"This language is very old. Can you read it?"

"No. But I got an app for that. If you type the words in, it will translate them into English, or French, or Dutch, or something. So, that's what I did. Sometimes a word didn't translate to English, it would translate to Swedish. Then, from Swedish, it would translate to French or Dutch. I'd translate it 'til it got to a language I thought was close enough. The translated words are on that paper I gave you."

"And you combined it with the other spells and said it about fifty times."

"Yeah."

"We have a place to start." Morning took the papers.

Day joined his brothers at the other table.

Aubrey watched the vampires pull out laptops from black bags under the table. He was not even aware they had them. Then, they went to work. He listened for a moment and then realized he didn't understand what they were saying.

* * * *

"Emma, darling." Night took her napkin from her lap and placed it in her bowl before she pushed red liquid way. "I will answer any questions you have, but you must promise to never use these spells again. Do I have your word?"

Emma grabbed the dishes from the table, placed them on an empty table across from them, and shook her head. "Yes. I wasn't trying to cause any trouble. I just wanted to get the prize money to get me a new iPad. I cracked the screen on mine and Daddy won't get me a new one. That's why I'm working here, to get the money. Do you mind if I record what you say? I have to make the presentation next week and may not be able to get all the work done again. But if it's recorded, I will have it for the presentation. Unless you can come as my proof."

Pushing the book further back on the table, Emma pulled out her cell phone and found the app for voice recordings.

Night watched the girl work at removing the dishes and settle on the table top again. "Humans don't take kindly to vampires mixing with children; there are many tales that we eat children." She threw Aubrey a sideways glance. "If the program is at night, I will see what I can do. Shall we get started?"

Emma gasped. "Do you really eat children?"

"No. Neither I nor my brothers would ever hurt a child. Let's get started."

Emma smiled. "Sure. To start with, your first name is Night. What is your last name?"

"Star."

"To be clear, you are not the first vampire, but you know the first vampire and how he was made. Right?"

"Yes. I am not the very first vampire, I am the number three vampire. My brother, Sky, was the number two vampire. My father was the number one. My father's name is River. He is the first vampire ever."

Excitement danced all over Emma. "Wow! You're the first woman vampire! How old are you?"

"I only learned to count a little over five thousand years ago. But we had been made long before I could count."

"Do you know where your father is now?"

"Yes. He sleeps. He and my mother have been sleeping for about three hundred years, more or less."

Emma frowned. "How is that done?"

"They simply decided they needed a rest from this world and willed themselves to sleep. They have done this before and will wake when they feel it's time."

Aubrey said, "Lot's of stuff has happened in the last century or two. TV, airplanes, Internet, cars. Lots of stuff."

Night's voice stayed soft and musical, but her words were matter of fact. "Yes, they will be surprised when they wake. But they will adjust."

Emma was barely able to contain herself. She wiggled and rocked back and forth on the table. "How did your father become a vampire?"

"In his youth, he married a witch. During his marriage to the witch, he married my mother and had to hide my mother from the witch. This witch had much power. My father believes to this very day that the witch cast spells over him to make him marry and stay with her.

"In those days, when the men went to battle, a witch cast spells that helped them win the battles they fought. After a battle, the practice was to kill all the men and steal the women. They would bring the women back to be slaves, and when food was in short supply, they became food. In one of those battles, my father found my mother. When he took her back to his home, she was pregnant with my brothers, Earth and Sky. So, he found a cave and made a home for her."

"This was during a time when people respected witches. Having a witch in your midst was considered a good omen. Her place in the community or what we would now call a community was welcome. It wasn't 'til much later that people feared witches and sought to kill them.

"My father said he always feared the witch. He had seen her go out in the night into the open field and call for a spirit to come to her. Many times, they did come. They made her magic strong. Because of her magic, my father became a great man. He was tall in stature and a fearless warrior. He killed many and brought home the spoils, which he divided between the witch and my mother."

"But where ... how did she get the spirits?" Emma asked with wide eyed interest.

"Darling, spirits are everywhere," Night said and waved her hand artfully in the air. "From the beginning of time, they have floated through the atmosphere, going nowhere in particular. I believe that most of them are mindless, just floating to whatever lies before them, while others are seeking. What, I have no idea. But when something captures their attention, they investigate and then move on their way. Some can be called and harnessed, be it for good or bad, depending on who is doing the calling."

Wonder filled Emma's eyes. "Were there a lot of them?"

"There are lots of them. Some float on the currents in the air, while others walk the shadows of the earth. Surely, you have seen movement in the corner of your eye, and when you turn, there is nothing there. Or maybe you feel as if someone is watching or listening to you, but when you look, you see nothing. Those are the ways of the spirits."

Emma's concentration was so intense, she squinted. "How do you get their attention?"

"Just call to them," Night said. "If you interest one, it will answer. But you must be very careful. Some of them are very dangerous, some of them like to play tricks, while some of them are looking for a home. All of them are unpredictable. Unless you have strong magic, you will not have their loyalty."

Aubrey didn't like the direction the conversation was going or the amount of interest Emma was showing in spirits. The last thing he wanted was to have Emma playing with unknown spirits. He asked, "That witch could command the spirits and she made your father love her?"

Night shook her head. "My father did not love the witch, and she had no children. She feared him leaving and not coming back to her, then she'd have to fend for herself. My mother gave birth to three more sons and my father found much comfort in her. My father knew the treachery of the witch and kept my mother and brothers hidden from her."

"Through the years, the witch was able to increase her magic by harnessing and controlling certain spirits. For instance, when my father was gone too long, she would send her spirits after him to bring him back to her. My mother said she could see the black shadow of the spirit on the wind 'til it finally surrounded my father and tortured him until he returned to the witch. But as soon as the spirit released him, he would go back to my mother. The witch didn't like that."

"My father watched the witch. After a while, he began to fear for my mother and brothers' safety. He told my mother about witchcraft as he watched, listened and learned so she could use it to protect herself. He taught her everything he learned. And we," Night nodded toward her brothers, "became my mother's apprentices."

"Eventually, the witch learned of the betrayal. So, she bargained with my father. She would release him once she had a child and he agreed. Men can be stupid. By that time, my mother had six children and she had none. Even I, as a newborn, knew the woman was barren, but she convinced my father to stay and she worked her magic."

Night shook herself. She pulled the corners of her mouth down and looked in the air.

Aubrey wasn't sure if it was for her father or the witch. Out of habit, he tried again to scent her, to get a sense of her feelings. Nothing. It was driving him crazy.

"My father said the witch cut herself with a silver knife and offered the bleeding wounds to a spirit she commanded. She then told him the spirits wanted his blood ... that it was to help her conceive. So, he allowed her to cut him with her silver blade and one of her spirits that craved blood entered my father and feasted on him."

"On the other mountain, my mother worried for my father. She had weak magic but strong love. All her spells were of love to keep her Master safe and to bring him back to her."

"You see, little witch, two women warred over the soul of one man, and in a way, they both won. Understand, we have no scientific facts, these are only our thoughts. The witch's blood spirit entered my father's body and drank his blood until there was none left. Before it could leave his body, my mother's spirits of life entered him as well. A wound on a vampire heals very quickly. We suppose that the spirits entered through the wounds the witch inflicted, then the wound sealed before the spirits were able to leave. The spirits found their respective places in my father and would not let him rest in death, but brought him to my mother. He was changed, but he was back."

Emma was wide eyed on the edge of her seat. "What happened to the witch?"

"Upon my father's first waking, he didn't know what was happening to him. The blood lust was strong, he could not control it. He needed to feed. By his own admission, he fed on the entire village, including the witch. Thus, ended the witch."

Night sighed long and thoughtful. "He didn't understand the changes in him—his fangs, his increased strength, his need to stay out of sunlight, the craving that only blood can satisfy. Everything was enhanced ... vision, hearing, the sense of smell, any and all appetites."

"He stayed away from us for a few days out of fear of hurting us. He didn't know how to control his thirst. But my mother kept casting spells that compelled him to come and he did. He explained to her what happened to him. Together, they worked out a way for him to stay close to the family and not do us harm. As a family, we worked out the obstacles."

Images of a prehistoric time filled Aubrey's mind. A man and a woman who were so in love with each other, they wanted to be together, no matter what. Love didn't go with his vocabulary. Experience told him love came and went without as much as a goodbye. He searched his mind for a better word ... devoted ... that fit better. A man and woman devoted enough to endure centuries with one another. Who wouldn't fight the Satan himself for that kind of relationship?

"Because there were only a few people in the world," Night forged ahead, "Father mostly drank the blood of animals. He brought meat home for us to eat, and we covered ourselves with the fur. We dug deeper in the cave we lived in to make sure he was out of the sun. During the daylight hours, we were extra vigilant to be sure no man or beast came near the cave. When the sun set and my father rose, with vampire speed, he'd leave us and only return when his appetite had been satiated. Then, he would settle into being my mother's mate and our father. That was my childhood. That was life as we knew it."

* * * *

She made it sound so simple, as if it was normal to be the daughter of a vampire. Then again, he was the son of a werewolf, and his species were as old as time as well. Even though he didn't know the history of werewolves, he figured it could have started pretty much the same. Aubrey was lost in thought when, out of nowhere, Tina brought a saucer with a melted Hershey bar on it. She placed the plate in front of Night, and then stepped back to the edge of the room.

"Why ya do that?" Aubrey demanded of Tina.

Tina looked confused. She opened her mouth but no words came out.

"I asked her to bring it to me," Night said coyly.

"I didn't hear you ask for that."

"I don't always use my voice," Night said sheepishly.

Night had to have used telepathy. Neither Aubrey nor his wolf liked that. It upset him that someone in his pack could be controlled mentally. "Use your voice from now on.

I'm having a hard time keeping up with things as it is." He didn't care how curt he sounded.

"As you wish, Pack Master." Night turned to her brothers and said, "May I have some blood, please?"

Night's words sounded innocent. The meaning almost escaped his reasoning and would have except the male vampire sitting closest to the table—Day, if Aubrey's memory served him correctly--bit into his hand, bringing forth a bright red flow of blood. He held it over the melted chocolate and let it flow until his sister said, "Thank you."

Night took her index finger and mixed the chocolate and blood together. With a seductive sweep of the hand, she placed the chocolate on her tongue. She blushed, an actual blush. Aubrey found that adorable.

Night said, "I love blood chocolate."

Curious, Aubrey said, "Are you eating? I thought vampires couldn't eat."

"I don't know if it's really eating. When I put it in my mouth, it dissolves into nothing. But the flavor of the chocolate gives the blood a little something extra. It burst on my tongue and it makes my insides smile. Would you like to try some? A little chocolate-flavored blood." She pushed the plate closer to him.

"No." His answer was more a command than anything. He saw her flinch. *Good*, he thought. Respect the wolf. He didn't want it to fester, and asked, "Your mother was a witch, too?"

Night swiped her tongue once more with the chocolate. "A witch made not born. She became one out of necessity." Her voice was still warm and friendly. He hadn't offended her.

Emma shooed him away. "You said your brother was number two. How did that happen?"

Night glanced at the table where her brothers sat toiling on their laptops and tablets. She waited until she got a quiet nod from Dark before she got on with the story.

"It was because of me. I was young and impetuous and not wanting to be minded. My brother, Dark, ordered me to come with him through the forest to our cave. I wanted to take the path and started running, forcing him to chase me, when I startled a bear. The bear was on me in an instant and would have killed me because I was young and small. My brother attacked the bear, though he had no weapons. All I could do was scream and run through the forest to call for help from my other brothers. My father heard my screaming and came to my brother's aid. He fought the bear and killed it. In the fight, the bear clawed my father. He had a gaping wound on his chest when he picked up my dying brother. He took Dark to my mother in the hope she had some magic to heal him. My father noticed my brother licking at the claw marks and drinking his blood. He asked my brother if it made him feel better, and he said yes. My father opened his vein and allowed him to drink as much as he wanted."

"Within minutes, he writhed on the ground in pain as the blood worked through his system, replacing his live blood with my father's vampire blood. We didn't know at that time what would happen. When he died, we all grieved because this was the first time any of us had ever experienced or witnessed the death of a loved one. My father was distraught, thinking it was his fault. But a few hours later, Day awakened craving blood. That's how vampire number two was made. Later, I was made followed by Earth, Day, Morning and Sky."

"Now you have the order. We are the first family. For the sake of this conversation and Emma, I am the first female vampire." Night smiled at Emma.

Emma danced in her seat and raised her hands to the roof. "Whoop, whoop! Girl power!"

Aubrey couldn't hold back a smile.

Emma frowned and said in a tiny voice, "How much does it hurt to turn into vampire?"

"Oh, little one," Night said with a deep frown. "Such pain I hope you never experience. It is like being sound asleep, then having your body dipped in liquid fire. It's acid burning through your blood a fraction of a centimeter at a time. You would vomit and convulse. Every hair on your body jabs your skin. Your sweat burns. Your eyes are on fire. Even your fingernails and teeth hurt you to the point you wish for death. Your heartbeat, your breathing, your hearing are beyond painful. You will give your very soul to make the pain stop. And it doesn't. There is no comfort, nothing that can ease the pain. There is no time limit on how long it will take."

"I wanted the transformation to kill me, but it didn't. When it was over, my body was whole. I was better, more perfect than I had ever been."

Emma looked at the table where the male vampires sat. "And it was like that for all of you?"

"For every vampire made," Earth said, his voice as smooth as silk.

"Within a few years, we were all made in the same way, having met our individual deaths in our own time and way. My mother was the only one that changed slowly over time. First, she became sensitive to sunlight. Then, she ate less and less food. When we were young, we didn't know why. As adults, we realize that taking vampire blood over an extended period of time will change a person and they will become a vampire. We came to the conclusion it happened because she drank my father's blood over time."

Aubrey's forehead creased. "If a person is not a vampire, why would they drink blood?" He wanted to appear neutral, but couldn't keep the disgust from his voice or his face.

"Vampire blood is magical," Dark said with a mischievous grin. "In erotic situations, it calls to your partner. The taste is intensified. It's sweeter, saltier, intoxicating, a drug. It is alive. You will experience sensations in your mouth that move throughout the body. In bed, it makes the experience more satisfying. Once you've tasted it, you will want to taste it again. My assumption is father helped mother with an injury of some sort. Afterwards, I'm sure he couldn't deny her request. These details are private between a man and his woman."

Emma checked her recorder. Satisfied it was still working properly, she asked, "What was it like once you were made?"

Night hesitated. She slid her hair from her shoulder, and then leaned on the table. "For centuries, we stayed on the outskirts. We lived in the forest, dug ourselves deeper in caves, and stayed away from the growing human population as much as possible. Our main nourishment came from animals, with the occasional person as a holiday meal. But in truth, we lived as we always lived—our clan together in caves, mistrusting of the world. That way of life was the only one we knew."

"After a while, I became a wanderer. I constantly looked for caves. In case someone discovered where we slept, we would have another place to go. Or, if we were caught out close to dawn, we could hide. As the population grew, I wandered close to cities and hunted on the outskirts. I had a problem with knowing when to stop feeding. My victims often died. One too many deaths and a whole village would become afraid. They were simple people and suspicious of anyone new, anyone different. I was never welcome."

Aubrey tried to put himself in their place. He could see it. "The first vampires were all in your family. How did it get outside of the family?"

"One of my brothers met a whore he decided he couldn't live without, only to find out later that he could."

Earth lifted his eyes and said in an even voice, "I lived, I learned."

Every man in the room nodded and chuckled in agreement.

"And on this point, the males bond," Night sighed.

Emma shrugged her shoulders. She faced Earth and asked, "Then what happened?" She reached for the recorder to be sure it was close enough to get what Earth was saying.

"As soon as she was made, she made another whore, who made another. I know this because in the early years whenever I encounter a vampire, I would inquire as to their maker and the path always came back to her and ultimately back to us."

"Now that other vampires were making other vampires, things were soon out of our control. Not that we realized we had control. Or at least, we didn't realize it until it was too late."

Turning back to Night, Emma asked, "Through the years, how many vampires have you made?"

"I made my brother and a baby I found, but she was a mistake. A pathetic creature that never developed and could not take care of itself. She was forever an infant and it was relief when she died."

"How did she die?"

"It was close to dawn and she would not come inside. I was too afraid of the sun to go outside. I watched her burn. I loved her and grieved much when she died."

Another thought came to Emma. She focused on Earth again. "Was that whore the first vampire you ever made?"

"No. I made Day."

Day gave that ever slight nod.

"Have you made a lot of others?"

"No, just two."

"I understand why you made your brothers. But why did you make a whore? Were you in love with her? Aubrey likes whores, too. How come you didn't find some nice girl to make?"

"Emma!" Aubrey shouted and looked around the room from one pack mate to another.

Todd was the only one to meet his eyes with a wicked knowing grin.

"That's what dad says," Emma shot back at her brother, and went on. "Did you love this woman and think she was going to be your wife?"

Earth locked eyes with Aubrey as if to ask a silent question if he should continue.

Aubrey shrugged.

"I was feeding from her, and she –," Earth weighed his words carefully, focusing on Emma. "She touched me. A woman had never touched me before. It distracted me enough to allow her to do as she pleased. She thought it would give her a few more minutes to live, and it did."

"You guys did it?" Emma asked.

"Emma," Aubrey snapped. "That's not appropriate."

"It's research," Emma retorted.

"She helped me realize that sex and drinking blood are very connected." Earth looked at his sister to gauge her reaction. As far as Aubrey could tell, there was none. "Up until that point, I had no idea."

"How does that happen? You a faggot?" Aubrey asked. His interest piqued.

"During my life, I never saw a woman. I never touched one nor was touched by one."

One of the wolves at the back of the room said, "How the hell do you go your whole life without seeing a woman? They're everywhere."

Aubrey knew the voice belonged to the diner's cook, Chester. He looked in the reflective glass for confirmation, and then noticed there were no customers left in the diner.

Earth answered. "There were not many people on earth back then, not like they are now. During my entire mortal life, I may have seen ten people, all of them male. The concept of a woman outside of my mother was not exactly new, but it was foreign. When I was first made, my thirst was a driving force and people were a delicacy. When I got the chance to have a person, all I could think was to drink. If this woman had not touched me, she would have never gotten my attention and in a matter of seconds, she would have been dead. She was very cunning. Her name was Hune."

"You made her a vampire after that?"

'No. I shared her with my brothers. After that, we'd look long and hard for more women. Now, women are not hard to find."

Emma's frown alerted Earth that she didn't like his answer. "Why did you make her a vampire?"

"She asked me at just the right moment and made the compelling argument that sex between two vampires would be even more ... enjoyable."

Aubrey cringed and dreaded what Emma might say next. He never considered himself a prude, but discussing sex with Emma in the room unnerved him.

Earth considered his words for a second. "I made her, taught her what I knew, and when she thought she knew enough, she left. I didn't see her again for a very long time. When we met again, I had to kill her."

Emma's mouth dropped. "Wow, you killed her. Why?"

"She set herself up as some sort of god and had her followers try to kill my sister. The choice was simple. She had to die."

Loyalty. They were loyal to each other. Aubrey noted another pack trait in the vampires.

"It was through Hune's death I met the man that became my educator. His name was Cornelius. He took me to his home and changed my life." Excitement filled Night's voice. "Emma, darling, I'm sure you take these things for granted, but until that point, I had spent my entire life living in caves, sitting in dirt and mud. I was a filthy creature who had never had a bath. This man gave me my first bath. Emma, this experience is so significant to me, I have never forgotten it and I could live it over and over."

Night squealed and clapped her little hands. The sound was so feminine, it made Aubrey's wolf jump. The wolf liked that sound, liked the joy in her eyes, and the wonder on her face. Both halves of Aubrey waited in anticipation to hear the sound again. Aubrey looked at the woman who sat before him. He tried to imagine her dirty and covered in mud. He found himself wishing he'd been the one to give her that first bath.

She sounded so ... so girly. Aubrey liked girly. He liked to see women in dresses and high heels. He liked sniffing women, smelling their powdered skin, locating the perfume they put on their pulse points. He liked curls. He enjoyed the way they bounced when they walked, beckoning him to bound after them.

Night went on. "We got to know each other and I learned that after he was made, he did exactly the same thing we did. He went back to the life he lived before. He was a teacher, a philosopher, and a debater. He hosted great parties in his home and was known throughout the community as a great man.

"This fascinated me. I watched him carefully and learned from him about how to be a part of the community. I wanted to learn because I had no intention of going back to live inside a cave ever again, and I never have. Emma, darling, this is important because to this day, there are vampires that live in caves who have never come into modern times. It is more difficult than you think to leave what you know to be safe and step out into the unknown. As it was for my family, we stayed in caves for centuries before we got the courage to try to come out. There are many things to learn. But the hardest lesson to learn is not to kill when you feed, to learn it's better to take a little from a lot than to take too much from one. It's a very, very hard lesson to learn, but I learned. We all did. Now, it's not really a concern. Through time, everything has an opportunity to change, and here I sit in a public place with a bowl of synthetic blood, having a discussion with werewolves."

"How time has changed," Aubrey said taking a long pull on his beer.

Emma shuffled her papers as she rearranged them in some sort of order. She checked her previously written report. Pulling out a pencil from her pocket, she made marks on the paper. "I'm checking to be sure I've asked all the questions I said I would ask."

All eyes fell on the girl. Her innocence was so pure it was difficult to find fault in her. Aubrey realized his anger with his little sister was gone and he had a sliver of pride in her. She had no fear of the vampires even though he and the rest of the pack considered them unpredictable at best. Her purpose was solid, direct. Her determination carried out with a will of iron. A true werewolf. He made the decision right then and there he would buy her the iPad himself.

A question flashed in Emma's eyes. "Do you all live together?"

"Sometime," Night answered.

"Do you keep all of your coffins in the same room?"

"We have no coffins." Night said. "We were created during a time when coffins didn't exist. When we lived, if you died, you died. You were dragged off to where the stench and insects didn't affect anyone. If you were eaten by animals, so be it. I can't tell you when I first saw someone cover a body with dirt and I thought how strange that was. Even to burn the body was strange to me. Then, it became more and more common for loved ones to say their goodbyes in such a manner. Besides, if you drink enough blood, you will change, no matter what. So, a coffin is not needed, nor is there a need to be buried. Well, if it's close to dawn and you are outside, you will need protection from the sun. Other than that, any dark place will do. Basement, closet, doesn't matter, as long as sunlight can't penetrate."

"Night," Sky said. "We have the translation."

Night took Emma's hands in hers. "Are you ready to cast another spell, little witch?"

"Really? Just like that?" Emma asked, surprised.

"Just like that," Night said with a reassuring smile. "Are you frightened?"

"No," Emma said. "I'm not ready for you to go."

"Oh," Night said, her voice low and enchanting. "We are not going just yet. First, we dance."

"Dance?" Aubrey asked. "What are you dancing for?"

"It's part of the magic," Night said, and asked Emma, "Surely, you danced when you first cast your spell?"

Emma stammered, "I guess. I don't know. Well, maybe. I like to dance and I do it all the time."

That was an understatement, Aubrey thought. Emma was always hopping and jumping around, calling it dancing.

"As do I, little witch, tonight we dance." Night clapped her hands.

Aubrey listened for a moment as the vampires conversed in a language he didn't understand. Aubrey became uneasy. Again, he tried to scent the vamps. All he got was the scent of pack: *Apprehension, mistrust, lust, relief, fear, excitement, lust, amusement, curiosity and more lust.* He looked in the mirrored glass and saw that Ashley and Hillary, two human females from the kitchen staff, had

83

joined them. The girls were all smiles as they stared at the table of good looking men. It didn't matter to them that the men were vampires.

He could scent nothing from the vamps. Once again, his wolf became agitated. Having a scent was a natural thing. He checked his inner wolf, mentally reminding him that these vamps were older than anyone they had ever encountered. The wolf calmed and went back to watching Night. His wolf liked her. Hell, the man liked her. Aubrey had the overwhelming desire to touch her, but he knew that would not be considered acceptable.

"What language do you speak?" Emma jumped off the table.

"It is our first language. I don't think it has a name. I don't think I have ever heard anyone outside our family ever speak this language. It is what our parents spoke to us and we have never forgotten it." Night shrugged and gave an off handed wave. She tucked her left hand under her chin and rested her elbow on the table.

Aubrey liked how she moved—fluid, graceful, feminine.

Again, he found himself comparing Night against his female counterparts. Most of his female liaisons were with the wolves of his pack or a neighboring pack whenever they got together. Most female wolves were long and slender, their bodies straight and flat with strong arms and legs. Their breasts were rather small—none larger than a C cup. Though werewolves were of all nationalities, most of them were born with light brown hair regardless of where they came from.

Night was short, compact, and full of soft curves that made her seem all the more woman. From his height, it was easy to peek at the mounds of flesh that were her ample breasts. He wanted to touch her.

Without conscious thought, he reached for her left arm and rested his thumb gently on where her pulse should have been.

Stillness filled the air, drawing the attention of his wolf, crouched at full alert. Everyone, everyone, vampire and werewolves, alike fixated on him. Even Emma watched and wondered what he was doing.

What was he doing? Aubrey wondered to himself.

In an effort to cover himself, Aubrey reached for the bracelet Night wore. Little charms decorated golden links. He picked up one. Engraved on the little heart was the word, "Sister". He chose another charm. Also a heart engraved with the same word, "Sister". There was a larger heart charm and it was engraved with the word, "Daughter". The next charm he picked up was a square with a heart in the middle, and the word "Lover" was inscribed on it.

His eyes shot up to meet hers.

"I have recognizable skills," Night lifted her eyebrows.

Aubrey lifted his eyebrows and leaned closer. "I'll have to find out."

"Night, we have the translation," Day repeated in a much sterner tone. "We should go outside and complete this task."

Night didn't pull her arm away from Aubrey. She looked at him with sultry eyes. "Pack Master." Night called his name soft and sensuous. Aubrey hoped no one else heard her. Reluctantly, he let go of her arm.

"Pack Master, shall we depart?"

Aubrey stood up, pulling his long legs together. "I'll follow you."

Night slid her arm under his and together they started for the front door. Her touch was gentle and cool on his bare skin. With his left hand, he motioned toward the front door in an old world manner. Together, they stepped toward the door.

Aubrey heard one of the brothers' call Night's name sharply, speaking that weird language that was their own.

Night responded to her brother in the same language. Earth's voice stopped the conversation when he ordered Night, "You will obey."

Aubrey felt his arm drop abruptly. Night looked at him and shrugged, then reached for Day's hand and laced her fingers with his. Day looked at his hand and frowned but didn't pull away.

Night taunted her brother by batting her eyes and giving him a sly smile. Day turned his head away from Night but didn't release her hand.

Earth and Sky moved in front of Night and proceeded to the door. Day took the position next to Night and followed the first two, Morning and Dark flanked from behind.

Aubrey recognized them as sentinels protecting their queen. A pack move. He liked that.

Emma hurried past Aubrey to hold Dark's hand as he walked out the door.

Aubrey allowed his temper to flair. "Emma," He rumbled. He wanted to be sure Emma recognized his agitation. He was more than a little put off that the vampires didn't want him touching their sister, but felt it was okay to touch his.

"We have to dance," Emma yelled over her shoulder and sped up in an attempt to pull the vampire with her.

Aubrey had no choice but to follow. When he got close enough to grab her, Emma scurried away.

Dark's reprimand was smooth and low. "Little witch, your brother has concern for you. And rightfully so, this is a most dangerous night."

Aubrey stopped, shocked the vampire was taking his side.

Emma whined, "He never likes me to have any fun."

Dark's voice remained neutral. "Your brother has much love for you and seeks to protect you. Often, what seems fun will take your life. We are vampires, little witch. Through the centuries, we have killed more people than we can count. We came to this place tonight with intentions of killing the one that was disturbing our father. If we had found deceit, it would not have mattered that you were a child. It is your innocence that has saved you. Your safety has been the primary concern in your brother's mind. He is prepared to die for you tonight. You are fortunate to have someone like him to watch over you."

Emma pulled her face tight. "How do you know?"

"It is my gift. I read intention. I know thoughts. You cannot deceive me. Your thoughts are clear to me before you even know they exist."

"He likes your sister," Emma blurted.

"He is male. She is beautiful. However, if you are thinking he will choose my sister over you, you are wrong. He is prepared to die for you, just as I am prepared to die for my sister. You are being a bad girl. You should stop, now."

Aubrey could tell there was compulsion in the subtle command. Emma let go of Dark's hand and moved closer to her brother. "Sorry."

Aubrey's big hand came down to palm her small head. He gave her a gentle squeeze and pushed her toward the door. "Let's get this over with."

Together, Aubrey and Emma stepped through the door into the parking lot. Instantly, Aubrey's wolf sensed danger. The outside air, thick and heavy, reeked of something strange that Aubrey couldn't identify. He could only describe the smell as cardboard. As far as his eye could see, a heavy layer of fog shrouded everything.

Aubrey looked deeper. There was more than one layer of fog. He was able to count at least four. "What in the world is that?"

"Magic," Dark said from a few feet away.

"What kind?" Emma asked.

"Our intent is to put an end to this thing tonight. In preparation, we covered this place with a spell to keep people away. And to keep those who chance to escape in."

"So, I don't have any business inside tonight because you are keeping people away?"

"Yes. We will compensate you for the loss," Earth stated.

Arrogant bastards, Aubrey thought. "What happened to the people inside that left?"

"They went to wherever they desired. The fog would have only kept them if they were somehow deceiving us. Since they were not, they were able to go wherever they wanted."

Aubrey became fully aware how unprepared he'd been for this encounter. These vampires had strolled into his business with a purpose. They had planned for all contingencies. He thought back on how they entered two-by-two going in different directions before they settled in the small dining room.

Looking Dark in the eye, Aubrey asked, "Did you do something on the inside of my diner?"

"We spelled the inside to get the people out of the way. They enjoyed their meal, paid, and left. We wanted only people involved to witness."

"Witness what?" Aubrey straightened to his full height. He wanted Dark to know he would not be easy prey. He'd protect Emma and his pack mates with his life.

Aubrey looked around to see who else had come outside. There were the human females, Ashley and Hillary. Pack mates, Carla, Tina, and Shannon were in place. His hang out buddies, Todd, Nick, and Darla had his back. Also, the pack enforcers, Chester and Bucky were in the mix. Finally, the reason for all this attention, Emma, was present. They were pack, full-blooded werewolves; the horror in the night, their combined strength unequaled among mortal men. Together, they could walk through a war zone and come out without a scratch.

"This is some weird bull," Chester said to Aubrey.

Todd came to his other side. "I don't trust this. Something strange is going on out here."

Aubrey decided not to hold back. "Witchcraft. They covered the property with it before they came in. They did the same thing inside. That's the reason we were slow tonight."

The fog swirled above the ground crawling through the men's legs, moving on to where the women were gathered. The women chatted and seemed unaware of the night, the stillness, the quietness, the promise of something lurking. Aubrey looked toward the end of the lot. From the spot where he was standing, he could normally see the traffic signal on the main drive and the endless flow of traffic. Tonight, he couldn't see past the fog, nor could he see any traffic at the other end of the street. He lifted his eyes to the sky, only to see the heavy blanket of fog above him, thick and low. They were surrounded.

Looking down, Aubrey saw the fog swirl around his boots. He was sure he saw tendrils reaching up his leg, reaching for him. He lifted his boot and stomped, sending the swirl scattering for just a second before it settled around his boots again.

"I don't like this," Aubrey said. "Can't you get rid of this fog?"

"It will go on its own once we have completed our task," Sky said from a few feet away. "It won't be long."

"It gives us privacy," Night offered with her seductive smile. "I prefer not to have prying eyes. No one will be able to see or hear what we say or do. We are totally covered from the rest of the world."

"So, when I say I see layers of fog, I'm right?"

Night nodded.

"And what's that I see moving in the fog?"

"The fog responds to intentions. If your thoughts and feelings are pure, it will not bother you." Night gave a dismissive wave of the hand as if that level of fog was the most natural thing in the world.

Lights came on inside of a huge hulking black truck parked several feet away. Music filled the air.

"Hey, you have to turn that down," Aubrey shouted over the volume. "This is a quiet community. The people around here work. They don't like loud noise."

"No one can hear outside the fog. They cannot see inside the fog, hear what's going on inside the fog, or come inside. This place only exists for us." Night gave him a wry smile. "We should get started."

Dark sat in the black truck and inserted a CD, filling the air with what Aubrey could only describe as classical music. Aubrey winced, as did the other members of his pack.

"Don't worry. It will get better," Night said from her post beside him. "You must understand, spell casting requires a mood. There are steps to preparation."

Not knowing what to say, Aubrey nodded.

"Sky, as always, you will listen," Night instructed. "Earth, you will dance with us and keep the flame. Day, you will cast with Emma and me."

Each brother nodded as his name was called out.

Everything they did, every movement they made, let Aubrey know they had done this sort of thing before. It made him uneasy. He'd always avoided magic. People that indulged in that sort of thing made him nervous. That was the very reason he hadn't been seeking a replacement for the shaman. Those sort of people did things. They said things.

Things that made him leery. Worse, they made his wolf uneasy. Right now, both man and wolf were anxious.

Aubrey felt the ripple under his skin. The wolf was ready. No, not ready. The wolf needed to come out; just in case. In case of what? He didn't know. He loosened another button on his shirt and worked his feet in his boots to make sure they were loose enough not to get in his way should the need for him to change arrive.

Energy filled the air. Aubrey looked at Chester, who stared back at him. Darla removed the flannel shirt that covered her tank top and crouched low to the ground. Everyone held their breath.

"Emma, darling," Night cooed. "Together, we will make a circle with this salt."

Aubrey saw two boxes of salt in Night's hands. *Where the hell did they come from?*

"Emma, dear, go in one direction and I the other. We are going to make a circle. It should be large, big enough for us to dance in. All right? We will stop when our ends meet."

Emma nodded and took one of the boxes of salt.

Night gently placed a hand on the girls' shoulder. In a louder voice, she said to everyone else, "Only those involved in the ritual can be inside the circle. Once the circle is made, you cannot come in and we cannot come out until the ritual is complete."

Tension built strong in Aubrey. He rolled his neck and shoulders. He tried to relax. He felt his control slipping away. He was responsible for Emma. "Emma, come here." He barked out the words.

"What?" Emma stomped her foot.

"Now," he roared. His wolf was dominant and overwhelming. It was the reason he was the Alpha. He was Pack Master.

Poking out her bottom lip, Emma slinked to her brother. "Why?" she whined.

"I don't want you to do this."

"But I want to."

"No," he said in a tone that could not be challenged. "Give her back her salt and go inside."

Emma's face crumpled. Her large eyes that had been filled with wonder and excitement instantly filled with tears. She turned to Night and extended the box of salt.

"Pack Master," Night said. Her voice a satin caress he felt it all the way to his toes. "This must be done in order to protect Emma."

"I'll protect her."

"You cannot. It is very, very dangerous to wake a vampire. This vampire has been asleep for three hundred years. He will rise angry and extremely hungry. He will be compelled to follow the witch's magic and come to her. She does not have enough skill to protect herself. And you yourself have said you have no shaman or witch for your pack. She will be helpless and at his mercy. Because he is my father, I would like to believe he would not hurt her because she is a child. But he is vampire. In the trance of magic, he may not be able to recognize that she is an innocent. He may only scare her. He could kill her. He might feel bad later, but she would be dead just the same. And what of you, Pack Master? How would you feel if these things happen just as I have said? To live your life knowing that you had the chance to save your sister and you didn't take it because of your mistrust. Pack Master, it is best we complete this tonight."

Aubrey listened. Night's voice was soft, compelling. Hell, she might be using magic on him right now. He forced himself to stop looking at Night and turned to Nick, his friend since childhood.

Without being asked, Nick said, "She's right, Bra. If what she says is true, we'll all be looking over our shoulders for this vamp to come. And you know we'll all die protecting our pups. It could be bad, man. Really bad."

Aubrey looked at each vampire in turn. He was well aware of their strength and speed. They had power he could not even imagine. In his life, he'd met a few baby vamps that were still learning their new lifestyles. But these were ancients. Their lives and skills honed to perfection. The fact that they existed now, thousands of years after their creation, was proof of that.

Tina chimed in. "They could have come in here, made a ruckus and tried to take what they wanted. Instead, they came in and gave you respect, acknowledging you as pack master."

Aubrey wanted to discount Tina's words since he knew the female vamp could control her. But the words were true, regardless of who had spoken them. He prided himself as a man of reason, logical in his thoughts. But this was Emma. The closest thing he had to a child of his own.

There was so much to consider. And a lot going on in this little company gathered in the parking lot of his diner. Werewolves, witches and vampires. Not to mention whatever the hell was lurking in the fog.

"Aubrey, I'm gonna be okay." Emma held his hand. "You're here to look after me, and you never let anything bad happen to me. But I wanna do this. This will give me life experience for my Lifestyles class. That's a solid A in two classes." Emma lifted her brows to the top of her forehead and held up two fingers, her eyes imploring him to consider the possibilities.

The little minx was going to use school to get her way. Emma knew how Aubrey felt about education, that it was the answer to having a better life. The one thing he really wanted for her. Not the life he had with his father following construction jobs around the country, living in seedy hotel rooms, going to school for only a few weeks a year.

Not to mention his dad's drinking and romping in the woods with both werewolves and feral wolves. His dad's motto was "Somebody's got to keep the race alive."

Emma's mother wasn't much better. She was an uneducated waitress who worked in truck stops and followed Aubrey's dad around to fight with him. Neither parent had much regard for education, didn't see any value in it at all.

That wasn't what Aubrey wanted for himself. As soon as Aubrey was old enough, he went to trade school and on to business school. He worked construction full-time and part-time in the diner while he lived in his truck. When he raised enough money, he purchased the diner from the previous owner, when he was ready to retire.

When Aubrey discovered his dad had a new woman and they had a child, he offered to take care of Emma so she could go to school on the regular and have better choices than most werewolf children. Emma had been with Aubrey since she was three-years-old. Even though his dad and her mom came to visit every few weeks, Emma was his. So she just didn't get it. None of them got it. His heart couldn't take it if something happened to Emma.

Never, under any circumstances, could Aubrey deliberately put Emma in harm's way, no matter his apprehensions. This had to be finished tonight. He inhaled deeply and blew out the breath slowly allowing an audible sigh.

Emma knew that sigh. She wrapped herself around her brother with several excited hops. "Thank you. Thank you," she squealed. Releasing him, she ran back to Night. "Okay, I'm ready."

Together Emma and Night popped the seals on the boxes of salt. "Walk in the opposite direction, sprinkle an even layer as you go," Night said.

Without a word Emma followed her instructions. Together they walked creating a circle with Day as their center.

Day lit a candle. Again Aubrey wondered. He hadn't seen any candles earlier. Nor had he seen matches. But there the candle was, lit and shinning, as bright as a single flickering candle could.

Aubrey watched Day turn in small slow circles as the salt spilled from the boxes to the ground. Day murmured low ancient words Aubrey didn't understand. He didn't know a freakin' thing about witchcraft but he knew that this thing, this pouring of salt, this murmuring was significant.

Within a minute, Night and Emma were standing side-by-side with only a small gap between the salt. Night filled the gap. She took the boxes and sat them on the ground near the salt and said. "It is begun."

All the male vamps gave a slight bow of the head.

Night took off her shoes and instantly dropped several inches in height. Aubrey couldn't help but notice she was only an inch or two taller than Emma. Night pulled off her jacket and unwound the scarf from her neck and shoulders.

She dropped the clothes in a pile near the boxes of salt. "Emma, darling, you should take off your clothes."

Emma looked shocked. She whirled around to see Day pull his shirt over his head and tug at the drawstring on his shorts.

"NO!" Emma screeched.

Night and Day froze.

"No, I don't want to take my clothes off."

"That's it," Aubrey snapped and started for Emma. He raised his foot to step over the circle of salt and instantly the circle burst into flames four feet high, just as something pulled him back. Aubrey turned ready to tear the head off whoever had pulled him. Shocked he saw only a tentacle of fog seeping back into the mist.

Fury seized him. The hand that pulled him back was solid and strong. Aubrey couldn't stop himself from letting a warning howl fill the night.

107

"Pack Master," Night called to him from behind the flames.

Aubrey was angry with himself, but even angrier with Night and the whole situation.

"Pack Master, it is all right. Emma is safe." Night looked at Day who did a pressing motion with his hands. The flames lowered as if someone had turned the dial on a gas tank. Now there was only an inch of fire that burned around the circle.

Aubrey could feel himself losing it. He was sure the fire would leap as high as he could jump if he tried again to get into the circle. But he could not; no, he would not allow his little innocent baby sister to dance naked with a grown man in public, much less a vampire. He started to pace, his wolf close enough to the surface he could feel fur break through his skin.

"Pack Master," Night called again, her voice smooth and soft. "Calm yourself. Nothing will happen to this little one. Not here, not tonight."

Aubrey stopped. He leaned forward ready to pounce. "Why should I trust you?" he demanded. "Give me one freakin' reason."

"Because you are not dead," Night said just as candidly as she had said everything else. "We wish you no harm. We wish Emma no harm. Calm yourself. This will be over shortly." With a hand she beckoned to one of her brothers. "If you allow Morning, he will help you to be calm."

Aubrey looked for the vampire where he had last seen him by the truck. When he located Morning, he was less than two feet from Aubrey. Why hadn't Aubrey seen him move?

"I don't want to take my clothes off." Emma stated again, her arms protectively crossed over her budding breast.

"Of course, not." Night said. "The nudity is more about freedom then being naked. Can you move freely with your clothes on?"

Emma nodded.

"Then we shall keep our clothes on. Perhaps, if you pull your shirt out of your pants and take off your shoes and socks, so you will be connected to the earth. Are those things acceptable to you?"

Emma nodded and bent to take off her shoes. When she had her socks off, she stuffed them in the shoes and placed them near the salt and gave Aubrey a nervous glance.

For the first time, Aubrey saw worry in Emma's eyes.

Aubrey's heart sank, so heavy it seemed filled with lead. He wanted to howl. Hell, he wanted to roar like a lion and bring the heavens down. But his throat was closed, the sound catching.

"I'm okay." Emma tried to reassure him with a weak smile and a wave of her fingers.

"Pack Master." Earth's voice seemed close to his ear. But when Aubrey looked Earth was still in the same place some feet away from him. "If Emma is worried for you, she will not be able to give herself totally to the dance or concentrate fully on removing her spell. She must be single-minded. I am listening. I hear what has not been said. Your sister is protected; of this you have my word. And my word is law. Tell her you are fine."

Aubrey felt the pressure in Earth's voice, stroking, soothing, caressing. He wanted to fight, to do what he did best, tear someone limb from limb. But he needed to calm himself and let this thing come to an end.

"Go ahead, Emma," Aubrey said despite his dry clenching throat.

Night pulled Emma by the hand and gently swayed to the music allowing her fangs to show as she threw back her mass of dark hair and lifted her arms to the night sky.

Marvin Gaye's, "Got To Give It Up" filled the night air, followed by Robin Thickes', "Blurred Lines". By the time Nelly's, "It's Hot In Here" played, the tension was defused between werewolf and vampire. Heads bobbed and feet tapped to the rhythm of the beat. The human women and female wolves stripped off their shirts littering the parking lot as they shamelessly gyrated in front of the male vamps and rubbed up and down the hard bodied males.

Aubrey watched Emma dance rhythmically to the beat of the music. He had never seen her dance before, not like this. Flinging her arms in the air and her feet shuffled from one place to the other. Her small hips swung from side-to-side. She smiled, sensing nothing but the joy of dancing. Aubrey relaxed a fraction.

The music changed to an alluring, soul thumping, drum beat, the cadence mysterious and compelling. It called to Aubrey, made him think of hunting prey—not just any prey, human prey with blood pounding hard, laced with adrenaline and tainted with fear. The human knowing that death was stalking and there were only moments if not seconds left to live. The drum tweaked his senses, making him expectant and dreadful at the same time.

Night stopped dancing. She walked seductively toward Aubrey, her full lips curled in a sensual grin. Both man and wolf regretted neither would get to see her naked and dancing by firelight. Night stopped at the salt ring and picked up a box of salt. Giving Aubrey a sly wink, she danced back to Emma and stood for a moment allowing the music to saturate Emma who flung her head carelessly from side-to-side.

"Emma, darling," Night said, drawing the girl's attention." It's time to remove your spell." Night took

Emma's hand, turned her around, and then set her dancing in the opposite direction they had been dancing originally. After a few times around the circle in the opposite direction, Night filled Emma's hand with the salt. "Say your words, little witch, while letting the salt fall from you hand. Time your words exactly so the last word falls with the last grain of salt and this will bring an end to your spell."

Emma obeyed. She spoke softly, letting a pinch of salt fall with each word she spoke. Night poured more salt into the top of Emma's hand and encouraged her to continue by repeating the words after Emma. Before long, Night and Day were chanting the words with Emma.

The music continued but anticipation dwarfed the sound. One-by-one, everyone stopped dancing and focused on Night and Emma. By the time a box of salt had filtered through Emma's hand, the entire crowd knew and chanted the words along with Emma as if their chanting would help to make the intent stronger.

Emma opened her empty palm when she said her last word and let the remainder of the salt fall to the ground. She looked expectantly at Night.

"Blow what remains on your hand to the winds to be carried swift and far."

Emma did as she was told. She blew the palm of her hand upward and out taking the last granules of salt from her. As soon as she finished blowing the salt, the circle of fire blazed with flames that jumped at least six feet before dying to a modest two-foot flame.

"It is done." Night took both of Emma's hands. "Your spell is broken. Now, let us ensure our vampire rests until he decides to wake for himself. Hold my hand. Together we will walk backward around the circle. I will say the words and when you have learned them, you will say it with me."

Emma nodded. With Night on one side of her and Day on the other, she walked backwards around the circle listening to the incantation.

Within seconds, the three in the circle were joined by those outside the circle repeating the incantation in an unspoken desire to seal it. When the trio got back to their starting point, they stopped. Day put the candle in front of Emma and instructed her to blow. The instant the flame went out, a swirling wind ascended on them.

The wind whipped Aubrey's hair in his face and eyes reminding him once again he needed a haircut. Aubrey saw the wind pick up the end of the salt trail and lift it in to the sky pulling the burning granules off into the night.

Every head lifted skyward watching the salt travel with lightning bolt speed. Within seconds, the salt was gone, blended in with the distant stars that covered the night.

Slowly, the fog closed the canopy once more.

"This is not good, Pack Master." Night faced Aubrey.

"What?"

"The fog should have gone after the salt. But it remains. "

"What does that mean?" Aubrey didn't even try to contain his frustration. He could feel panic starting again.

"There is treachery," Earth's voice was as smooth as silk.

Outraged, Aubrey issued a challenged. "Treachery? What are you talking about? I've been on the up and up with you from the start." Aubrey's mind raced. If for some reason this thing failed and they tried to remove Emma from his property, it wouldn't matter if the fog was there or not. There would be blood.

"It is not you, Pack Master," Earth said. "It is the one the fog clings to."

Looking to his right, Aubrey spotted Todd. His face contorted in an odd expression as he swatted at the mist that glided past him again and again. "What is this stuff?" Todd asked. "I think it likes me." Todd gave a slight chuckle and batted at the wispy tentacles.

Earth spoke in his usual soft manner. "I listened to his thoughts and have given the fog permission to have him."

Todd brushed at the fog. It became more aggressive, wrapping around him from face to neck.

Incensed, Aubrey declared, "I make all the decisions for my people."

"His evil is oily, the stench is foul. At the mention of Emma dancing naked, he dropped the shields on his mind. As we speak, he is attempting to devise a plan to take Emma. He is waiting for a chance to steal her away to do the unspeakable. He has taken at least four girls. I counted them as they passed through his thoughts. His perversion outweighs his good sense and his mind is uncontrolled, though he wishes to hide it from you, Pack Master. He should not be allowed to live, not only for Emma's sake, but the sake of all. Give the word and we'll let the fog consume him."

Aubrey was stunned. But then again not really, he knew deep inside it was true. How many times had Todd commented on little girls? Talked about the way they dressed – that dress is too sexy for her or made a statement about their bodies – she's gonna have a killer body when she grows up. Aubrey would look and just see a little girl and never gave it a second thought, but there was always an unusual scent Aubrey couldn't identify because it was so foreign to him. Now that it was said plain for him, he couldn't ignore it.

Todd walked through the mist toward Aubrey. "This stuff is stickin' to me like glue," he said, swatting at mist that swirled seductively around him.

"Yeah, and it's gonna do it for a while. The vamps told me you stalked Emma. That you like little girls. The vamp said he counted four in your head. They also told me that the fog would follow you and kill you. Good luck with that."

Aubrey scented Todd. *Surprise, fear, annoyance, anger.*

Aubrey's wolf was out before he could sensor himself. His eyes changed and his muzzle grew long. His canines grew and his tongue thickened, claws sliced through his skin and fur sprouted.

Todd jumped back, knowing he was no match for Aubrey in human form or wolf. As he retreated, Todd bumped into Chester and Bucky who were also ready to tear into him. The scent of pounding blood drew the attention of the rest of the pack along with the vampires. They, too, surrounded Todd and waited for Aubrey's signal.

Dark spoke up, a wicked grin on his face, "Pack Master, allow the fog to have him."

Aubrey had just enough awareness to hear Dark call his name. He paused when his gaze fell on Emma, her eyes wide with fear as she clutched Night in horror. Emma had never witnessed a true wolf attack.

"Remember the fog," Earth said close to his ear even though he was on the other side of the wolves that surrounded Todd. "It has power to deal with such treachery."

Aubrey remembered. The hand in the fog that pulled him back from the fire was strong and solid.

Pacing, Aubrey regained his control. For Emma's sake, he wouldn't allow the attack. He allowed himself to slowly calm and ordered his wolves to stand down. "The vamps have something in the fog. I say let whatever it is have him."

Shannon had already changed into her wolf form and howled her disapproval.

"I'm Pack Master. You obey me. Whatever is in that fog touched me earlier. It's strong and solid. I believe it can do the job."

"You are making a mistake," Todd yelled. "Who you gonna believe? Me or some SOB that's been dead for a billion years? They are controlling your mind, Aubrey. You know me. I would never do anything to Emma. I love her."

The smell of Todd's lies was rancid. The wolves gagged at the stench.

Aubrey turned to his former friend. "I hope it takes a long time to kill you. That you suffer, you sorry son-of-a-bitch. You are no longer pack. No longer do we eat meat with you. We no longer hunt together. We are brothers no more."

Todd looked around at the rest of his pack mates. Hatred filled their eyes as they all turned their backs on him and started toward the dinner. Without another word, Todd got in his car and drove away. A tiny vapor of fog followed Todd to his car and attached itself to the tailpipe of the Ford Galaxy as it rolled out of the parking lot.

Throughout the parking lot, the fog began to dissolve. Aubrey could see the traffic flowing on the main street as the cars streamed through the traffic stop. Above his head, the thick blankets of fog dispersed into a billion particles and floated upward to join with the stars. Aubrey looked to his left when the music that blasted from the big black truck suddenly stopped, leaving only the sound of car tires peeling on asphalt on the nearby boulevard.

Sky handed Aubrey an envelope, "Three thousand dollars. It should cover for the loss of business this evening."

"Dude, that's more than enough." Aubrey stuffed the envelope in his pocket and watched the male vampires pile into the truck. He took Night's elbow and escorted her to the passenger side of the truck and opened the door, relieved that this thing was over, but sorry Night was preparing to leave. He wanted to get to know her better. Maybe even find out where the blood feud between werewolf and vampire started. Find out if either one or both of them could overlook it long enough to get to really know one another.

A car rolled into the parking lot followed by another. College students spilled out, loud and oblivious to the happenings only moments before.

"Little witch, if my father should awake during your life time, I will ask him to meet with you. After all, he is the first, and that's what you really wanted."

"Ok," Emma said with a long sad face. "I'm glad you came. I hate for you to go. Thank you for helping me with my school work."

Night gave Emma a slight nod then whispered in her ear for a few seconds.

"I don't want to wait that long to see you again," Aubrey said, using his low, sexy voice. "You know, we could have a bowl of blood together sometime."

"Then, I say until I return, Pack Master."

And with that Night was gone.

* * * * *

Aubrey rolled his shoulders and stretched his neck from one side to the other. He wanted to bay at the setting sun. Something was calling to him. Not to him but his inner wolf. The wolf wanted out, was demanding to be released. But he couldn't allow it, not just yet. Later he promised—later.

But the wolf wouldn't be appeased. Aubrey flared his senses as far as he could. Nothing. That made him uneasy. He trusted his wolf. It could sense more than the man could, so he always allowed freedom and trust. Aubrey decided to take the wolf's anxiety as a warning. Something was happening.

Walking to the back door of the kitchen, Aubrey stood for a few seconds, tasting the air. Nothing, just the smell of rotting vegetables waiting to be picked up by the trash men. Again, he scented as far as he could. Nothing came back to him. He took one final look around before he decided to go inside. Just as he turned to go inside, he saw a bundle of fog hovering at the corner of the parking lot nearest the sub division. He watched it for a moment or two motionless. Waiting.

The fog didn't move.

Why should it? It was fog. Aubrey looked to the sky to see heavy clouds not only above Timberwolves, but across the city sky. Seemed normal. Ever since that night with the vampires, he didn't look at fog the same. Aubrey could still see the way it swam around and clung. He knew about the way it followed Todd and later tormented Todd. Todd had called Aubrey at least two dozen times begging Aubrey to have the fog leave him alone.

Todd described things to Aubrey in those calls. A clump of fog always stayed with Todd no matter where he went. A hand Todd could see and feel pressed against his neck cutting off his air. Someone or something poked him at night when he tried to sleep. The thing had even started stabbing Todd with his own hunting knife.

There were several other incidents and after each one, Todd would call Aubrey and beg for forgiveness. It didn't matter. Aubrey would never forgive him for wanting Emma, not to mention the other girls that Todd had already harmed. Besides, Aubrey didn't command the fog, the vamps did. He had no idea how to reach them. Aubrey wanted to contact them ... at least he wanted to contact Night.

In the end, Todd took a shotgun and painted a wall with is brains. From the night the vamps put the fog on Todd until the night Todd ended it, was exactly one year.

That was ten years ago.

Since that night, Aubrey had only encountered one vamp. That was when Emma was fifteen. The vamp that showed up that night was so new, the scent of his decaying flesh had Aubrey nauseated. The blonde vamp interrupted Aubrey's poker game when he walked into the diner with Emma slung over his shoulder and demanded, "Who is pack master? I was told to give her to no one but the pack master."

Once Aubrey identified himself, the blonde male unceremoniously dumped a drunk Emma at Aubrey's feet, and then disappeared into the night. It wasn't until the next day when the morning news reported that some frat boys had gotten several underage girls drunk and date raped them. Emma had been part of that group, but somehow was spared.

Aubrey knew.

Tonight, there was something out there. It was in the air. His wolf was not letting go and Aubrey had learned a long time ago to trust his wolf. That trust had saved his life on more than one occasion. He'd just have to wait. In the meantime, there was business.

As soon as he opened the door to the diner, the outside world disappeared and the reality of doing business was shoved in his face.

The night went on without incident. The waitresses complained about the customers, the customers complained about the waitress. The cooks complained about the menu and Aubrey complained about them all. Business as usual.

By ten o'clock, the diner was devoid of customers. Not a single person remained. Unusual Aubrey went into the kitchen to check inventory and help break down one of the fryers. Then, he heard the waitress call back an order for two bottles of blood warmed in a bowl with spoons.

Aubrey knew that order. He pulled out his cell and texted Emma and followed the new waitress, Janice, out to the smaller dinning section to the round table in the corner. Janice nervously deposited her order.

"Pack Master," Night said with a hint of glee as the waitress retreated out of sight.

Aubrey closed his phone and slid it into his pocket. "Emma will be down in a minute."

Night smiled and extended her hand. "Of course, she will. Please sit."

129

Before he could reach the chair, Emma flew around the corner screaming, her ponytail flying in the wake she created. She was dressed in a pink Timberwolves's T-shirt that came to her knees and she was in her bare feet. As soon as she saw Night, she wrapped herself around her in an affectionate hug. "You're back! You're back!"

"When you didn't come to the lecture hall, I thought you had forgotten me. I got an A on my report, but I didn't win. Alex Hall won the money. You know you changed my life. I've decided to be an activist for vampire rights. I'm going to work with the legislature this summer as a page. I'll finally get a chance to get out of this diner and do something meaningful."

"Then you are happy." Night worked her fingers between Emma's and clasped her hands. "At our last encounter, I left you a promise," Night said in a calm voice. Her eyes locked on Aubrey.

Aubrey hooked his thumbs in the belt loops of his jeans and leaned against the wall. "I told her."

"Emma, darling, this is my mother. Her name is Shai."

The woman was beautiful with dark, caramel skin and black hair coiled on top of her head. Her almond-shaped eyes were brown and calm.

Emma squealed and pulled the woman's hand from the table. "It's so good to meet you," Emma gushed."

Confused, Shai looked at Night before she allowed the touch.

Aubrey looked around the diner. Empty. He focused on the outside glass. It was covered with a thick layer of fog. He had to ask. "Is there going to be more spell casting tonight?"

"No," Night said. "I just like to take precautions when we are all together in one place. The fog has served me well for quite a while."

Emma gave an ear piercing scream. "You're him, aren't you? You're the first, the very first." She grabbed the man by his shoulders. "OMG, you look exactly the way I thought you would. Aubrey, he's here. The first one is here! I didn't notice you at first 'cause you all look so much alike. But I know it's you."

The vampire stood. It seemed to take forever for him to unfold to his full height. He had to be at least seven-feet tall. His black hair dusted his shoulders and accented the hard angles in his face. His posture was tall and straight. Aubrey knew he was witnessing a warrior of old.

Emma couldn't stop squealing her excitement.

"Emma, darling, this is my father. He is the first vampire created.

The vamp extended a hand, something that vampires almost never did.

Emma looked around to see who else was watching. Aubrey knew she was going to brag for days, no years. She finally turned her full attention to the tall vampire and took his hand.

He said, "I am River. I am the first."

THE END

11:50 p.m.

01 October 2015

Discussion Questions

1. Why didn't Aubrey know his sister was a witch, or did he know and just didn't want to say?

2. When Night was leaving she whispered something in Emma's ear. What could she have possibly said that could not be said out loud?

3. Do you think Aubrey and Night have real chemistry? Could they build a lasting relationship despite their cultural differences?

4. Do you think you could overcome any fears you have of vampires to accept them into normal everyday life?

About The Author

Monique Bowden Guice attended Indiana University and Barry University. Presently, she is working on several books including the next story in this series. Monique plans to write and publish in several genres.

Currently, she lives in Tallahassee, Florida, with her husband. She has one child. Monique is a member of the Tallahassee Authors Network and the Writers Workshop. She would like to thank both groups for their continued support of her writing.

She can be reached at mbguice@gmail.com and http://mbguice.webs.com/.